Virgil Hauselt Memorial Junior Academy

427 Capitola Road   -   475-4762

Santa Cruz, California 95060

This is
THE MAKE-IT ROOM
of Mr. & Mrs. Bumba

When Mr. Bumba and Mrs. Moon become
Mr. and Mrs. Bumba, exciting adventures
are sure to follow.

Read all 10 books
— written by Pearl Augusta Harwood

A LONG VACATION for Mr. & Mrs. Bumba

THE RUMMAGE SALE and Mr. & Mrs. Bumba

A SPECIAL GUEST for Mr. & Mrs. Bumba

THE MAKE-IT ROOM of Mr. & Mrs. Bumba

A THIEF VISITS Mr. & Mrs. Bumba

A HAPPY HALLOWEEN for Mr. & Mrs. Bumba

NEW YEAR'S DAY with Mr. & Mrs. Bumba

THE CARNIVAL with Mr. & Mrs. Bumba

CLIMBING A MOUNTAIN with Mr. & Mrs. Bumba

THE VERY BIG PROBLEM of Mr. & Mrs. Bumba

You will also enjoy . . .

the Mr. Bumba books

Mr. Bumba's NEW HOME
Mr. Bumba PLANTS A GARDEN
Mr. Bumba KEEPS HOUSE
Mr. Bumba AND THE ORANGE GROVE
Mr. Bumba's NEW JOB
Mr. Bumba HAS A PARTY
Mr. Bumba DRAWS A KITTEN
Mr. Bumba's FOUR-LEGGED COMPANY
Mr. Bumba RIDES A BICYCLE
Mr. Bumba's TUESDAY CLUB

the Mrs. Moon books

Mrs. Moon's STORY HOUR
Mrs. Moon AND HER FRIENDS
Mrs. Moon's POLLIWOGS
Mrs. Moon's PICNIC
Mrs. Moon GOES SHOPPING
Mrs. Moon's HARBOR TRIP
Mrs. Moon AND THE DARK STAIRS
Mrs. Moon's RESCUE
Mrs. Moon TAKES A DRIVE
Mrs. Moon's CEMENT HAT

THE MAKE-IT ROOM

of Mr. and Mrs. Bumba

by
Pearl Augusta Harwood

pictures by
George Overlie

published by
Lerner Publications Company
Minneapolis, Minnesota

International Standard Book Number: 0-8225-0124-4
Library of Congress Catalog Card Number: 74-156357

Second Printing 1972

One morning when Bill looked over his fence into Mr. and Mrs. Bumba's yard, he saw something new.

Mr. Bumba was carrying some lumber from the station wagon. He was putting the lumber into a pile beside the garage.

"Are you going to build something, Mr. Bumba?" called Bill.

"Yes indeed, indeed I am," said Mr. Bumba, smiling a wide smile. "And I could use some help piling these boards."

Bill went over right away. "I do like to pile up boards," he said. "My, but you bought a lot of lumber."

Pretty soon Jane looked over her fence. "Is there something I could do to help?" she asked.

"Sure thing," said Mr. Bumba. "I can use all the help I can get. I am building a Make-It Room onto the garage."

"A Make-It Room!" said Jane and Bill together.

"Make what?" asked Jane.

Mrs. Bumba came out of the kitchen. She was wearing her working slacks and her working sweater.

"It's a Make-It Room for me," she said. "Mr. Bumba has his sun-room where he paints his pictures. And I need a room for a lot of things I am going to do very soon."

"You mean you're going to make things?" said Bill.

Mrs. Bumba nodded her head.

"What sort of things will you make?" asked Jane.

"Things out of clay," said Mrs. Bumba. "Things out of yarn. Things out of copper. Things out of rocks. And other things."

"Whew!" said Bill. "All those things, ALL AT ONCE?"

Mrs. Bumba laughed. "Well, maybe not quite all at once," she said. "I shall need a loom for weaving cloth, and a machine for polishing rocks, and an oven for firing clay. And a place to put all the things I use."

"And tables to work on," said Jane.

"And a sink for cleaning everything up," said Bill.

Lee came over from his house across the street. They told him all about the Make-It Room. He helped them pile up the lumber.

"What will you do with all the things you make?" asked Lee.

"Now, that is a very good question," said Mr. Bumba, smiling at Mrs. Bumba. "But I think Mrs. Bumba knows the answer."

"I know some gift shops that will take the things I make," said Mrs. Bumba. "Some of them are a long way from here."

"Will they buy everything you make?" asked Lee.

"They will take them," said Mrs. Bumba. "If they sell the things, then they will pay me."

"And if they don't sell them, they send them back to you?" asked Jane.

"So that you can try them in some other shop?" asked Bill.

Mrs. Bumba nodded her head.

"It sounds like a good business," said Lee.

"It will be lots of fun, anyway," said Mrs. Bumba.

"But first we must build the room," said Mr. Bumba. "And the wooden forms for the cement floor come first."

In a few days Mr. Bumba had the
cement floor made. A man came to help him
put up the frame for the walls and the roof
of the new room.

Whenever they could, Bill and Lee and Jane came over to help.

"You can all help nail the boards for the outside walls," said Mr. Bumba. "They will be just straight up and down. They are all twelve inches wide."

Lee looked at half a wall that was already up.

"Won't the rain come through the cracks between the boards?" he asked.

"Indeed it would," smiled Mr. Bumba. "But we'll nail on some TWO-inch boards over all the cracks!"

"Oh," said Bill, "I know what they call that. It's a 'board and batten' wall."

"Right," said Mr. Bumba. "Board and batten it is."

The roof slanted down from the garage roof. Some men came and spread hot tar over the new roof. Then they sprinkled green gravel all over it.

"I know what kind of a roof that is," said Lee. "It's a 'tar and gravel' roof."

"Tar and gravel it is," said Mr. Bumba. "My, but you boys seem to know a lot about building a house."

Mrs. Bumba was very pleased with the
room so far. "Now it is time to buy the
frames for the windows and doors," she said.

They had four windows and two doors
all ready to put in. They had come from a
house that was torn down.

Lee and Bill went with Mr. Bumba to buy the frames for the windows and doors. They came back without any frames at all.

"They don't make that size any more," said Bill to Mrs. Bumba. "Mr. Bumba will have to build all the frames himself."

"Oh dear," said Mrs. Bumba. "I don't like to have him do so much work."

"I don't mind," said Mr. Bumba. And in a few days he had the window frames and door frames all made. Then he set them into the walls.

Lee and Jane went with Mr. Bumba to buy the wide panels for the inside walls. They already had four panels that were left over from some other job. They came back without any more panels at all.

"We can't match those other panels anywhere," said Lee. "Mr. Bumba can have just one wall made with panels."

"Oh dear," said Mrs. Bumba. "What shall we do with the other three walls?"

"I guess I will use wall board and

plaster over it," said Mr. Bumba. "I don't mind plastering at all."

"One wall with panels and three walls with plaster will make a very pretty room," said Mrs. Bumba. "But I am sorry that you have so much extra work."

Next they had to get tiles to put on the cement floor. They had samples to look at. Jane and Bill and Lee helped Mr. and Mrs. Bumba decide which sample they liked best. They also had a second choice and a third choice.

All three of them went with Mr. Bumba to buy the tiles. They came back with several boxes. The boxes had different numbers on them.

"There weren't enough on hand of any of our three choices," said Jane, "so we got three kinds that go together all right."

"Mr. Bumba will have to work out a design, to make them all look right," said Bill.

"Oh dear," said Mrs. Bumba. "What a lot of work that will be!"

"I don't mind," said Mr. Bumba. "It takes an artist to make a design of DIFFERENT tiles! It will be fun."

After the floor was done Mr. Bumba built shelves all along one wall. Then he built a counter with cupboards under it. He put in a sink that he had been saving for a long time.

"Now we need a trap for under the sink, and faucets, and a basket sink strainer," he said.

Jane and Bill and Lee went with him to buy the plumbing. They bought the sink trap and the faucets. But the man did not have a basket sink strainer that was the right size.

"They don't come in that size anymore," he said. "Maybe you can find some other store that has one of that kind left over."

Mr. Bumba and Bill and Lee and Jane went to every store that sold sink strainers. No one had a basket sink strainer of the right size.

"Well, what if it doesn't have any strainer?" said Jane.

"Then you might lose all sorts of things down in the sink," said Bill.

"And stop up the pipes," said Lee.

They all sat in the station wagon and
thought and thought.

Then Jane said, "Isn't there ANY
OTHER KIND of a sink strainer?"

Mr. Bumba jumped up and got out of
the car. "Why yes," he said. "There's a flat
kind, without a basket. Maybe we could find
one of those!"

They all rushed into the store they had
just left.

"Why yes — plenty of them," said the man, when they asked for a flat sink strainer. "Why didn't you ask me that before?"

"We didn't think of it," said Mr. Bumba. "It was Jane here who had the idea."

"Now the plumbing can be all finished," said Lee.

"The Make-It Room is almost done," said Jane.

"Except it isn't painted yet," said Bill.

"That's right," said Mr. Bumba. "I will paint the outside, and Mrs. Bumba will paint the inside."

"Couldn't we help paint it?" asked Jane.

"Well, I guess you could," said Mr. Bumba. "One person could help me outside, and one person could help Mrs. Bumba inside."

"Then we could take turns," said Lee.

"I don't like the name 'Make-It Room,'" said Bill. "It should have another name — a real name."

"Like 'Bumba Bungalow'?" said Jane.

Mr. Bumba smiled a wide smile. "I think 'Bumba Bungalow' is the best name possible!" he said.

When everything was finished, Mr. and Mrs. Bumba asked Bill and Lee and Jane and their mothers and fathers to come over one Sunday afternoon.

The Make-It Room looked very pretty. Mrs. Bumba already had a lot of materials on the shelves for making things.

"These two long tables can be folded up if we want to have a big party in here," said Mrs. Bumba.

"But now, we can sit down at the tables and have ice cream and cookies," said Mr. Bumba.

"I wish WE had a Make-It Room in our house," said Jane.

"So do I," said Bill.

"So do I," said Lee.

Mrs. Bumba smiled at them all.

"Anyone who wants to make things," she said, "can come over here on Friday afternoons and I will help them."

"That's a wonderful idea," said Jane's mother. "I wish some of us were children, so we could come, too."

"Well," said Mrs. Bumba, "on Thursday mornings I could help any mothers who wanted to make things."

"Oh, WOULD you!" said Lee's mother. "I do want to learn to weave."

"And I do want to learn to make clay pottery," said Bill's mother.

"Looks as if the fathers are out of luck," laughed Bill's father.

"Well," said Mr. Bumba, "on Friday evenings I could help any fathers do woodworking."

"Hooray!" said Lee's father. "We'll be over next Friday!"

Then they all went outside to watch Mr. Bumba put up the new sign over the door.

It was a smooth, shiny piece of wood. On it, in big letters, was the name, BUMBA BUNGALOW.

Underneath, in letters almost as big, was written, EVERYBODY'S MAKE-IT ROOM.